The Cl...
by Bob It...
MG (4-8)
ATOS 5.8
1.0 pts
Non-Fiction

27898 EN

Inside the NFL

THE
CLEVELAND BROWNS

BOB ITALIA
ABDO & Daughters

Published by Abdo & Daughters, 4940 Viking Drive, Suite 622, Edina, Minnesota 55435.

Copyright © 1996 by Abdo Consulting Group, Inc., Pentagon Tower, P.O. Box 36036, Minneapolis, Minnesota 55435 USA. International copyrights reserved in all countries. No part of this book may be reproduced in any form without written permission from the publisher.

Printed in the United States.

Cover Photo credits: Wide World Photos/Allsport
Interior Photo credits: Wide World Photos

Edited by Paul Joseph

Library of Congress cataloging-in-Publication Data

Italia, Bob, 1955—
       The Cleveland Browns / Bob Italia.
       p.   cm. -- (Inside the NFL)
Includes index.
Summary: Provides an overview of the history and key personalities associated with the Cleveland Browns, a team that joined the NFL in 1950.
       ISBN 1-56239-536-X
1. Cleveland Browns (Football team) -- Juvenile literature. [1. Cleveland Browns (football team) 2. Football--History.] I. Title. II. Series: Italia, Bob, 1955— Inside the NFL.
GV956.C6I83   1996
796.332'64'0977132--dc20   95-43587
                                                                       CIP
                                                                        AC

CONTENTS

A Winning Tradition 4
The AAFC 6
Welcome to the NFL 8
Building a Dynasty 9
NFL Champions 10
Jim Brown 11
Life After Brown 14
Bernie Kosar 16
Vinny 24
On to Baltimore? 28
Glossary 29
Index 31

A Winning Tradition

The Cleveland Browns have one of the richest histories in the National Football League (NFL). In the 1950s, they won many division titles and championships. Some of the NFL's greatest players have worn Browns jerseys—players like quarterback Otto Graham and running back Jim Brown.

Since the birth of the Super Bowl in 1966, the Browns have not been to the championship game. A lack of a well-balanced team has hurt Cleveland's championship dreams. When the offense is good, the defense is lacking. When the defense is strong, the offense suffers.

These days, the Browns seem to be on the road to recovery. The offense is solid and the defense is improving. If quarterback Vinny Testaverde can play consistently, the Browns may find themselves playing for their first Super Bowl title.

Fullback Marion Motley (76) runs hard against the Los Angeles Rams in 1950.

**Opposite Page:
Wide receiver Mark Carrier catches a pass against the Arizona Cardinals.**

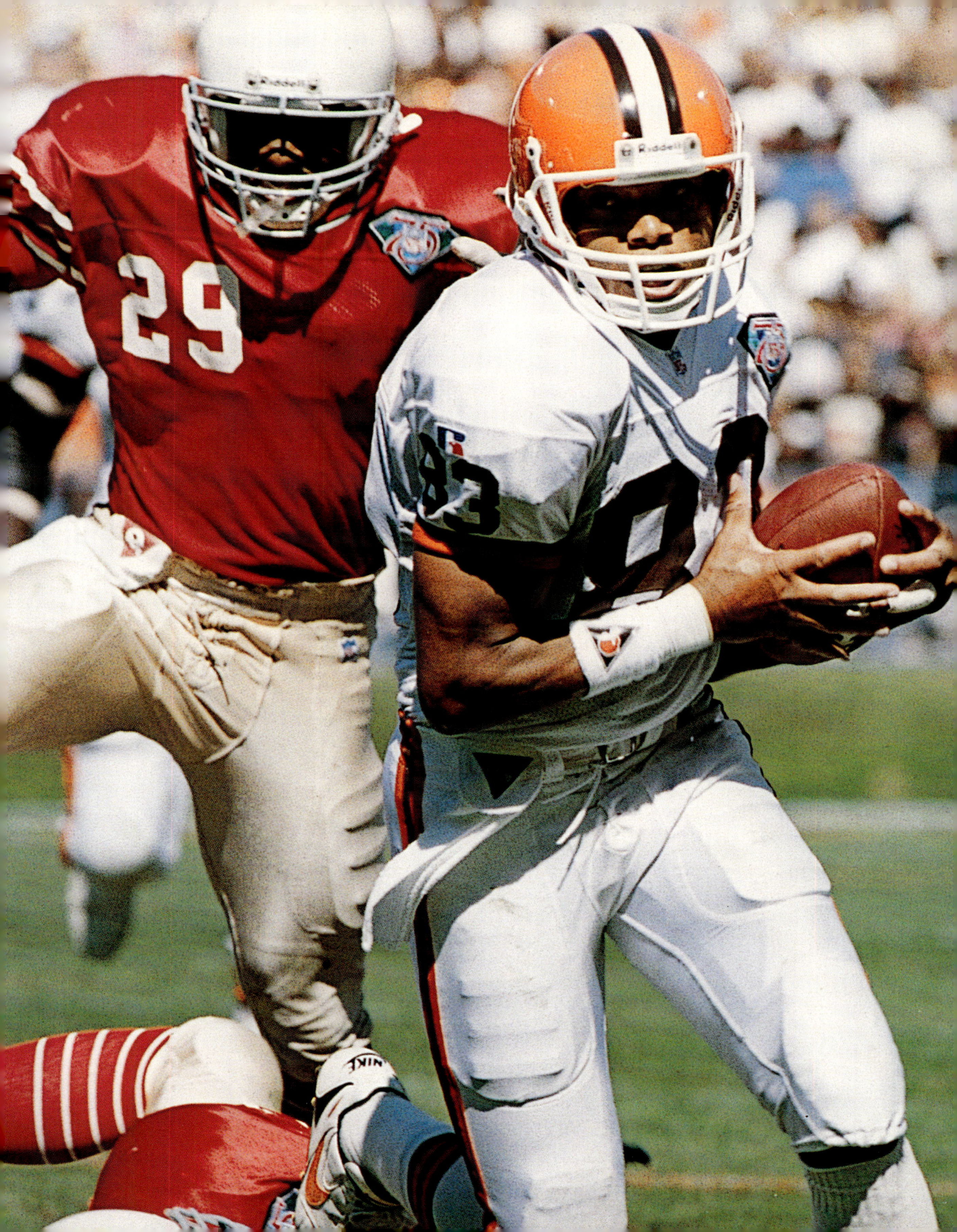
Riddell
29
Riddell
83

The AAFC

In 1946, the Cleveland Browns played their first season in the All-America Football Conference (AAFC). The Browns were the only champions in the four-year history of the league.

After the AAFC folded, its best teams joined the NFL. No one expected the Browns to repeat their success in the NFL. The National Football League teams was considered much better than the AAFC's. But head coach Paul Brown knew his team could play with anybody because of his quarterback, Otto Graham.

Quarterback Otto Graham spins for a touchdown against the Lions, 1954.

Dante Lavelli (56) is on the receiving end of an Otto Graham pass.

Graham began his career with the Browns in 1946 and led them to four-straight championships. But when he and his teammates joined the NFL, people wondered if he was good enough to win. Graham did not call his own plays. Paul Brown sent in plays with offensive guards, whom he rotated. At the time, it was not an accepted practice.

Welcome to the NFL

The Browns played their first NFL game against the Philadelphia Eagles in 1950. The Eagles were defending NFL champions, so the Browns would find out immediately just how good they were.

More than 70,000 people jammed Philadelphia's Franklin Field to watch the showdown between the two league champions. Eagles' fans expected Philadelphia to soundly defeat Cleveland. But Graham, fullback Marion Motley—the 240-pound fullback who was bigger than most linemen— and receiver Dante Lavelli put on an offensive show. When the game ended, it was the Browns who had done the pounding as they defeated the Eagles 35-10.

The Browns had a successful first season in the NFL. They surprised everyone but themselves as they won the league title in 1950—their fifth straight football championship. Cleveland returned to the championship game in 1951, but this time the Los Angeles Rams beat them 24-17. Amazingly, it was the first time in their 6-year history that the Browns *weren't* champions!

Fullback Marion Motley.

Building a Dynasty

Despite their first championship setback, the Browns were not about to give up their winning tradition. They won division titles in 1952 and 1953. But in each championship game, they lost to Detroit.

Still, the Browns were one of the NFL's most talented teams. Graham had two great receivers, Dante Lavelli and Mac Speedie. Dub Jones and Marion Motley spearheaded the running game. And placekicker Lou "The Toe" Groza was one of the most accurate in all of football.

Graham was the key to the Browns success. When he took the field, he expected to win every game. The Browns usually did.

In 1954, the Browns had an unusual start to the season. They lost two of their first three games and were in danger of not making it to the championship game for the first time in their nine-year history. But Graham rallied his team, and Cleveland won all but one of its remaining games. For the fourth year in a row, the Browns were Eastern Division champions.

Halfback Dub Jones (86) picks up speed as he runs for a touchdown against the Giants.

NFL Champions

For the third year in a row, the Browns played the Detroit Lions in the NFL championship game. The Browns were determined to win it all. Graham had one of his best games ever. He completed 9 of 12 passes for 163 yards and 3 touchdowns. He also had three rushing touchdowns.

As the game wound down, Brown removed Graham from the game. The 80,000 fans in Cleveland's Municipal Stadium gave Graham a standing ovation. Cleveland eventually won 56-10. After the game, Graham announced his retirement.

Brown tried to find a new quarterback for the 1955 season, but replacing Graham was an impossible task. Finally, Brown called Graham and pleaded with him to rejoin the team. Graham finally agreed.

Graham led the Browns to their tenth division title in ten years. In the NFL championship game, Graham guided the Browns to a 38-14 victory over the Los Angeles Rams. Afterward, he retired for good. He wanted to go out a champion, and he did.

Coach Paul Brown practicing with the 1952 Cleveland Browns.

Jim Brown

The Browns had won seven league titles in ten years. No professional football team had ever been so good for so long. But when Graham retired, Cleveland fans wondered if they would ever see such an outstanding player in a Browns jersey. Amazingly, it took only one year.

In 1957, the Browns drafted Syracuse University running back Jim Brown. The 6-foot, 228-pound Brown became an instant star. Not only was he one of the biggest fullbacks in the league, he was one of the fastest and strongest. When he could not run around defenders, Brown would run over them. To stop the Browns, defenses had to stop Jim Brown. It was not an easy task. Brown seemed indestructible, and he carried the ball often. Brown was the NFL's leading rusher nearly every season he played.

But with Jim Brown carrying the football, the Cleveland Browns could not find their way back to the NFL championship game. Frustrated with the sudden lack of playoff success, new Browns' owner Art Modell fired Paul Brown in 1962.

Paul Brown never got along with Jim Brown. But new coach Blanton Collier worked hard to develop a good relationship with the talented fullback.

The Browns set their sights on a championship in 1964. Along with Brown's running game, Cleveland had an explosive passing attack. Quarterback Frank Ryan often threw to two outstanding receivers, Gary Collins and Paul Warfield. Defensive end Doug Atkins anchored the defense.

The Browns were in first place most of the season. But losses to the St. Louis Cardinals hurt Cleveland's title chances. The Browns regrouped just in time to win their final game of the regular season, a 52-20 thrashing of the New York Giants. The victory earned Cleveland the Eastern Division title.

The Browns faced the Baltimore Colts in the championship game at Cleveland. The game was scoreless at halftime, but the Browns exploded in the second half. They scored 17 points in the third quarter on a Groza field goal and 2 Gary Collins touchdown receptions, then tacked on 10 more fourth-quarter points for a convincing 27-0 victory. It was their first league title since 1955. Brown gained 114 yards on 27 carries—most coming in the second half.

It looked as though the Browns could look forward to Jim Brown helping them win many more championships. But after the 1965 season, the 30-year-old Brown shocked the football world by announcing his retirement, stating the football part of his life was over. Brown left pro football as the NFL's all-time leading rusher. It would take 20 years before Chicago's Walter Payton would break Brown's yardage record.

**Opposite page:
Running back Jim Brown.**

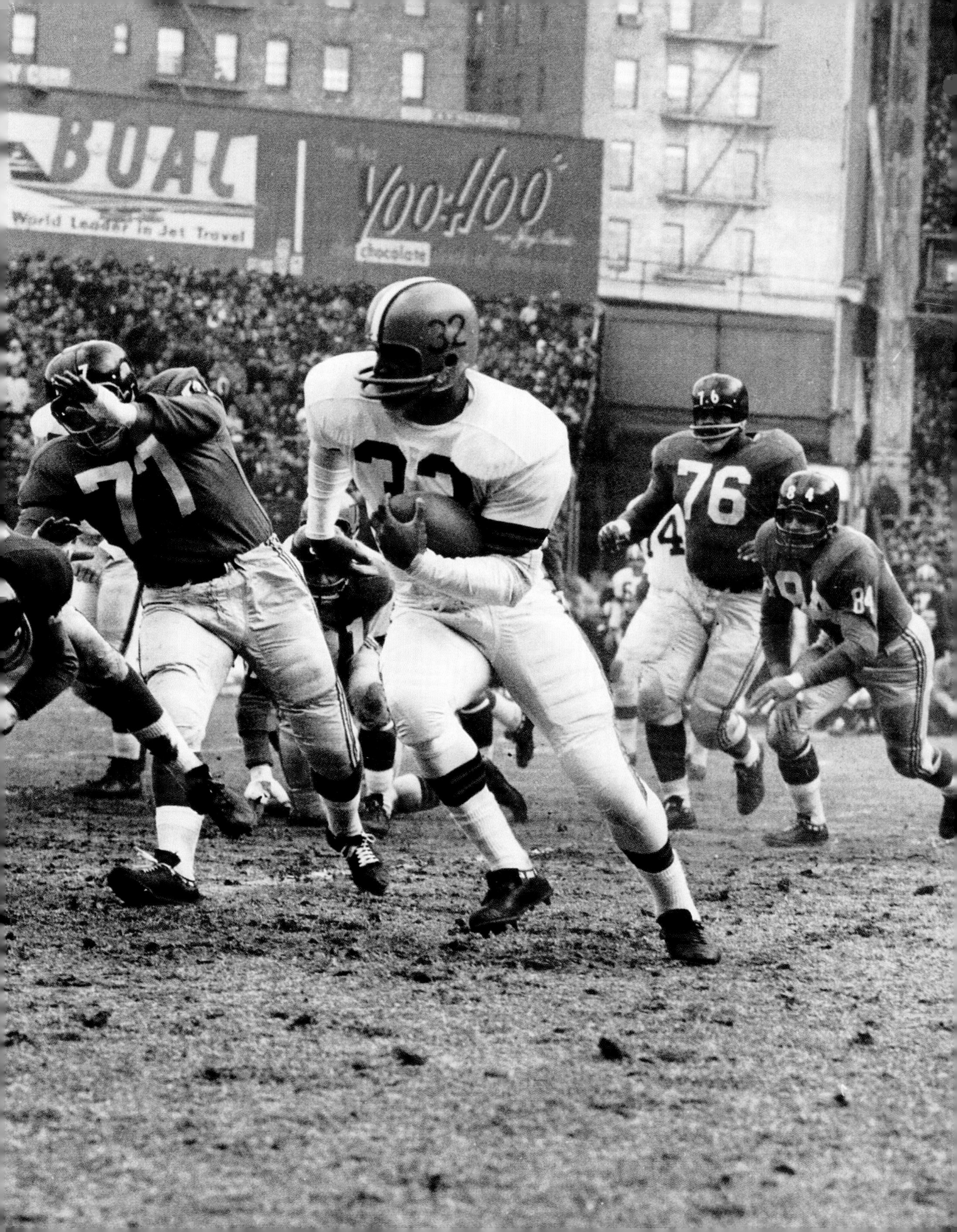
World Leader in Jet Travel
Yoo-Hoo
chocolate

Life After Brown

Though Brown retired, Cleveland still kept winning. Running back Leroy Kelly, wide receiver Paul Warfield, and quarterbacks Frank Ryan and Bill Nelson took up the slack and performed brilliantly.

In 1970, the American Football League and National Football League merged. The Browns joined the Central Division of the American Football Conference (AFC). Their division foes included Pittsburgh, Houston, and the Cincinnati Bengals.

Wide receiver Paul Warfield (42) fights his way through the Dallas defense.

In the early 1970s, Pittsburgh and Cincinnati built championship teams. The Browns often finished third in the division. Art Modell decided that a coaching change was in order. He wanted to find someone who would restore Cleveland's championship tradition.

In 1978, Sam Rutigliano replaced Forrest Gregg as head coach. Rutigliano rebuilt the team around quarterback Brian Sipe. Sipe struggled his first season. Cleveland fans were disappointed with his inconsistent play. But Rutigliano stayed with Sipe.

Toward the end of the season, Sipe settled down and played better as Cleveland finished 8-8.

In 1979, Sipe played like a seasoned veteran. With the help of wide receivers Reggie Rucker and Ricky Feacher, and tight end Ozzie Newsome, Sipe and the "Kardiac Kids" produced seven heart-stopping, fourth-quarter comebacks. Running backs Mike and Greg Pruitt provided stability in the rushing attack. Though they finished 9-7, the Browns did not make the playoffs. But because of their fourth-quarter heroics, greater things were expected in the following season.

In 1980, Sipe and the Browns did not let their fans down. They won the AFC Central Division title and earned home-field advantage throughout the AFC playoffs.

In their first playoff game, the Browns faced the Oakland Raiders. Late in the game, the Raiders held a 14-12 lead. But Sipe drove the Browns on a game-winning drive. With his team knocking at the goal line, Sipe dropped back to pass and looked for a receiver in the end zone. He lofted his pass, but it fell into the hands of Oakland's Mike Davis. Cleveland's season was over.

Bernie Kosar

Brian Sipe and the Kardiac Kids would never see the playoffs again. Unable to forget the disappointing loss to Oakland, the team stumbled through the next few seasons.

After the 1983 season, Sipe signed with the new United States Football League (USFL). Having suffered a 5-11 record in 1984, Rutigliano was fired. Marty Schottenheimer became the new head

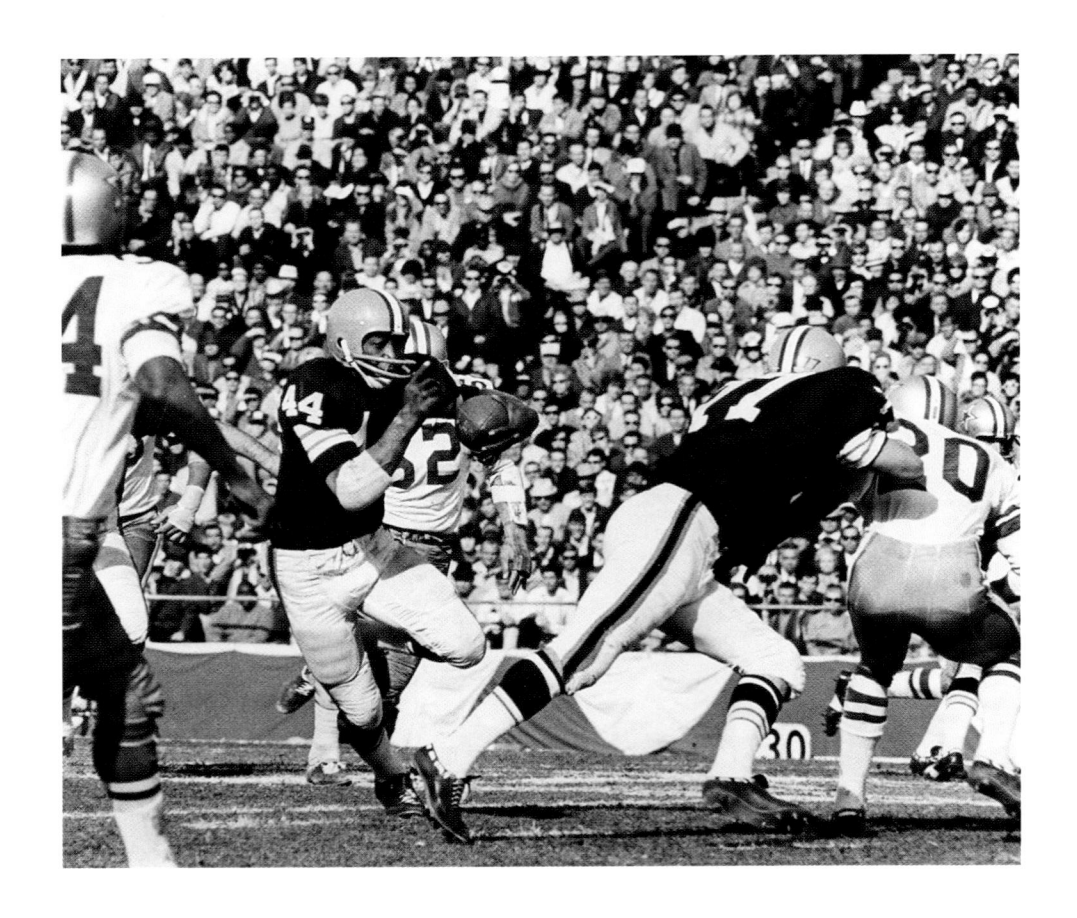

Running back Leroy Kelly (44) finds a hole against the Cowboys, 1967.

Quarterback Bernie Kosar, throws a pass during his rookie season, in 1985.

CLEVELAND BROWNS

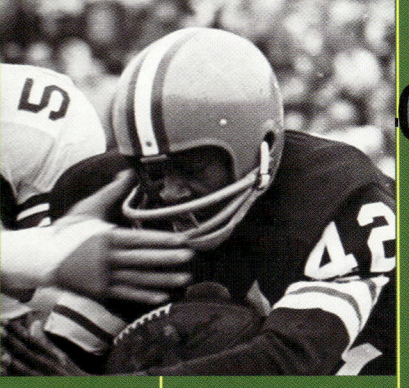

10   20

Paul Warfield leads the Browns to the NFL title game in 1969.

Otto Graham begins his career with the Browns in 1946.

CLEV
BRO

Marion Motley and the Browns win their first NFL game in 1950.

10   40

Bernie Kosar joins the team in 1985.

Vinny Testaverde becomes the starting quarterback in 1993.

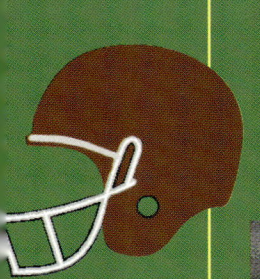

In 1980, Brian Sipe and the Browns win the AFC Central Division title.

CLEVELAND BROWNS

coach. His new quarterback was a young man born and raised near Cleveland. His name was Bernie Kosar.

Kosar starred at the University of Miami in Florida. When he graduated, Kosar wanted to play for the Cleveland Browns. The Browns picked him in the 1985 NFL Supplemental Draft, held a few weeks after the regular college draft.

Kosar impressed his new teammates from the very beginning. His intelligence and leadership abilities earned him the starting quarterback job.

Brian Sipe takes a snap in the shotgun formation against the Chargers.

Though they finished with an 8-8 record, the Browns won the Central Division title. Kosar often clicked with receivers Webster Slaughter, Brian Brennan, and Ozzie Newsome. Running backs Kevin Mack and Ernest Byner gave the Browns a potent rushing attack. On defense, cornerbacks Frank Minnifield and Hanford Dixon made the Pro Bowl. Linebacker Clay Matthews had one of his best years.

In 1986, Cleveland's 12-4 mark was the best record in the AFC. But in the playoffs, the Browns fell behind the New York Jets 20-10 in the fourth quarter.

Then Kosar led the Browns on two long drives. The first produced a touchdown and the second a game-tying field goal that sent the game into overtime. Cleveland got the ball and marched down the field. The game ended when Mark Moseley kicked a 27-yard field goal for the 23-20 Cleveland win.

In the AFC championship game, the Browns faced the Denver Broncos. The winner would earn a Super Bowl berth. Late in the fourth quarter, Kosar hit Brian Brennan on a long touchdown pass as the Browns grabbed a 20-13 lead. But the Broncos rallied behind quarterback John Elway, who drove his team to a tying touchdown with less than a minute left. Denver won 23-20 in overtime with a field goal.

It was a tough loss, but the Browns rebounded in 1987. They claimed the Central Division title once again and advanced to the AFC title game to meet the Denver Broncos for the second year in a row.

The Broncos took the early lead and built a seemingly insurmountable 31-10 lead in the third quarter.

But this time it was Kosar who rallied his team. Amazingly, Cleveland scored three touchdowns to tie the game at 31-31. Elway countered with his own scoring drive to make the score 38-31. But the Browns refused to give up. Kosar drove the Browns to the Denver goal line, but a fumble ended Cleveland's Super Bowl hopes.

Bernie Kosar goes back to pass against the Eagles, 1991.

In 1989, Bud Carson became the new head coach. He nearly led Cleveland to the Super Bowl. But for the third time in four years, the Browns lost to Denver in the conference championship.

Cleveland's future still looked bright. Kosar was only in his mid-twenties. The Browns' two outstanding wide receivers, Webster Slaughter and Reggie Langhorne, were also young. The team added a running back in Eric Metcalf, who complemented Kevin Mack's powerful running style.

The defense was also solid. Cornerback Frank Minnifield and linebacker Clay Matthews were among the NFL's best defensive players. Defensive lineman Michael Dean Perry was one of the league's best pass rushers.

But in 1990, the Browns suffered through the worst season in their history. They set team records for most losses and most points allowed. And they were shut out three times. Kosar was often rushed and was not effective. With little offense and a fading defense, Coach Carson lasted through nine games and seven losses. His replacement, Jim Shofner, went 1-6 before moving to the front office.

The following season, the Browns showed signs of life under new head coach Bill Belichick. They won four of their first eight games. But then injuries ruined their season as they finished 2-8 after midseason. Kosar had a good comeback season. Running back Leroy Hoard was the surprise player of the year by scoring 11 touchdowns, 9 of them on receptions. Kevin Mack joined him in the backfield and scored 10 touchdowns while rushing for 726 yards. The defense sliced its points allowed per game in half from the previous season.

In 1992, the Browns nearly made the playoffs. They were in the running entering Week 15, but then lost three straight games for their third consecutive losing season. The offense struggled all season because of injuries to Kosar. Todd Philcox and Mike Tomczak played adequately in his place. No Cleveland players finished among the conference leaders in any major offensive category. Linebacker Clay Matthews, the NFL's oldest defensive player, set team marks for longevity and career sacks.

Vinny

Quarterback Vinny Testaverde joined the team in 1993 which signaled the end for Kosar—even though he led them to a 5-3 start and first place in the AFC Central. Belichick, however, was not confident that Kosar's skills would last. On November 8, Kosar was traded to the Dallas Cowboys.

Vinny Testaverde throws a pass against the New Orleans Saints.

Because Testaverde was injured, Philcox took over. Cleveland lost three in a row and six of their final eight games to finish 7-9 and third in the division. When Testaverde did return, he threw more touchdowns than interceptions for the first time in his career. Running back Eric Metcalf had a league-high 1,923 all-purpose yards and two punt-return touchdowns.

Cleveland started the 1994 season with a 28-20 win over the Cincinnati Bengals. But after three weeks, Testaverde ranked last in the AFC in passing efficiency. He got better in Week 4 against the Indianapolis Colts, including a 65-yard strike to Hoard that won the game 21-14 in the fourth quarter. With the win, Cleveland moved to 3-1 and first place in the AFC Central.

In Week 8, the Browns rolled to their fifth consecutive win with a 37-13 victory over the winless Bengals. At 6-1, the Browns were off to their best start since 1963. Eric Metcalf returned a Bengals punt 73 yards for a touchdown—the fifth of his career.

The Browns faltered the next game, but then put back-to-back wins together. In a game against the Eagles, Hoard rushed for 86 yards, backup quarterback Mark Rypien threw a touchdown pass to Mark Carrier, and Matt Stover kicked four field goals. At 8-2, they led second-place Pittsburgh by one game.

With three weeks left in the season, the Browns were 9-4 and had fallen into second place. A Week 15 victory over the Dallas Cowboys lifted them to 10-4. The Browns used 4 Matt Stover field goals, 99 rushing yards from Hoard, a Testaverde touchdown pass, and 4 Dallas turnovers to surprise the Cowboys in Dallas. On the game's last play, Eric Turner fell on Cowboys tight end Jay Novacek before he could cross the goal line with the winning score. However, Pittsburgh also won to stay one game ahead of Cleveland. The showdown for first place was at hand.

In a Week 16 game at Pittsburgh, the Steelers seized a 14-0 lead and never let go. The 17-7 victory clinched the division for the Steelers. But the Browns still made the playoffs as a wildcard berth. To prepare for the playoffs, the Browns demolished Seattle 35-9 in the final week to finish the season at 11-5. But Cleveland fans wondered if Testaverde could lead the team to the Super Bowl.

In the regular season, Testaverde was the NFL's 22nd-ranked quarterback. In his career, he had thrown 32 more interceptions than touchdown passes. Even worse, he had never appeared in a playoff game.

In the first round against the New England Patriots, Testaverde was almost perfect as he led the Browns to a 20-13 win. Rolling out to

Running back Eric Metcalf (21) runs for a touchdown.

Browns receiver Mark Carrier catches a pass against the Falcons.

pass and scrambling when he had to, Testaverde passed for 268 yards with no interceptions. At one point, he completed 11 passes in a row. With the win, the Browns earned the right to play their arch-rivals—the Pittsburgh Steelers.

The Browns and Steelers had played a pair of close, hard-fought games earlier in the season, both won by Pittsburgh. But the Steelers won more easily this time. They scored on their first three drives for a 17-0 lead and stretched it to 24-3 at halftime before putting Cleveland away 29-9. The Steelers defense kept the ball away from Testaverde by rushing for 238 yards. They controlled the ball for more than 42 minutes.

On to Baltimore?

In 1995, the Browns got off to a good start. By midseason, however, they had fallen to 4-5 as Testaverde was benched.

But the news about Testaverde took a back seat to a much bigger event that occurred on November 7, 1995. That's when owner Art Modell announced he was moving the Browns—with the league's approval—to Baltimore for the 1996 season.

Modell did not sidestep the issue. The reason for the move, he said, was money.

"This has been a very, very tough road for my family and me," Modell told Associated Press reporters. "I leave my heart and part of my soul in Cleveland. But frankly, it came down to a simple proposition: I had no choice."

Baltimore offered to build Modell's team a $200 million stadium by 1998 and provide another $75 million for moving and improvements to Baltimore's Memorial Stadium where the Browns would play from 1996 to 1997.

Modell claimed that he had lost millions operating the Browns and was convinced the city could not match Baltimore's generous offer. But some observers doubted that Modell was losing money in Cleveland. He was moving the Browns, they said, to make even *more* money in Baltimore.

Fans were saddened and outraged. There was talk about court action to block the move. Others hoped to offer Modell a better financial package in Cleveland. But if none of these actions worked, the Browns would play their 1996 season in Baltimore—ending a rich 45-year NFL tradition in Cleveland.

GLOSSARY

ALL-PRO—A player who is voted to the Pro Bowl.
BACKFIELD—Players whose position is behind the line of scrimmage.
CORNERBACK—Either of two defensive halfbacks stationed a short distance behind the linebackers and relatively near the sidelines.
DEFENSIVE END—A defensive player who plays on the end of the line and often next to the defensive tackle.
DEFENSIVE TACKLE—A defensive player who plays on the line and between the guard and end.
ELIGIBLE—A player who is qualified to be voted into the Hall of Fame.
END ZONE—The area on either end of a football field where players score touchdowns.
EXTRA POINT—The additional one-point score added after a player makes a touchdown. Teams earn extra points if the placekicker kicks the ball through the uprights of the goalpost, or if an offensive player crosses the goal line with the football before being tackled.
FIELD GOAL—A three-point score awarded when a placekicker kicks the ball through the uprights of the goalpost.
FULLBACK—An offensive player who often lines up farthest behind the front line.
FUMBLE—When a player loses control of the football.
GUARD—An offensive lineman who plays between the tackles and center.
GROUND GAME—The running game.
HALFBACK—An offensive player whose position is behind the line of scrimmage.
HALFTIME—The time period between the second and third quarters of a football game.
INTERCEPTION—When a defensive player catches a pass from an offensive player.
KICK RETURNER—An offensive player who returns kickoffs.
LINEBACKER—A defensive player whose position is behind the line of scrimmage.
LINEMAN—An offensive or defensive player who plays on the line of scrimmage.
PASS—To throw the ball.
PASS RECEIVER—An offensive player who runs pass routes and catches passes.
PLACEKICKER—An offensive player who kicks extra points and field goals. The placekicker also kicks the ball from a tee to the opponent after his team has scored.

PLAYOFFS—The postseason games played amongst the division winners and wild card teams which determines the Super Bowl champion.
PRO BOWL—The postseason All-Star game which showcases the NFL's best players.
PUNT—To kick the ball to the opponent.
QUARTER—One of four 15-minute time periods that makes up a football game.
QUARTERBACK—The backfield player who usually calls the signals for the plays.
REGULAR SEASON—The games played after the preseason and before the playoffs.
ROOKIE—A first-year player.
RUNNING BACK—A backfield player who usually runs with the ball.
RUSH—To run with the football.
SACK—To tackle the quarterback behind the line of scrimmage.
SAFETY—A defensive back who plays behind the linemen and linebackers. Also, two points awarded for tackling an offensive player in his own end zone when he's carrying the ball.
SPECIAL TEAMS—Squads of football players that perform special tasks (for example, kickoff team and punt-return team).
SPONSOR—A person or company that finances a football team.
SUPER BOWL—The NFL Championship game played between the AFC champion and the NFC champion.
T FORMATION—An offensive formation in which the fullback lines up behind the center and quarterback with one halfback stationed on each side of the fullback.
TACKLE—An offensive or defensive lineman who plays between the ends and the guards.
TAILBACK—The offensive back farthest from the line of scrimmage.
TIGHT END—An offensive lineman who is stationed next to the tackles, and who usually blocks or catches passes.
TOUCHDOWN—When one team crosses the goal line of the other team's end zone. A touchdown is worth six points.
TURNOVER—To turn the ball over to an opponent either by a fumble, an interception, or on downs.
UNDERDOG—The team that is picked to lose the game.
WIDE RECEIVER—An offensive player who is stationed relatively close to the sidelines and who usually catches passes.
WILD CARD—A team that makes the playoffs without winning its division.
ZONE PASS DEFENSE—A pass defense method where defensive backs defend a certain area of the playing field rather than individual pass receivers.

INDEX

A

American Football League (AFL) 14
Atkins, Doug 11

B

Baltimore Colts 12
Belichick, Bill 23, 24
Brennan, Brian 21
Brown, Jim 4, 11, 12, 14
Brown, Paul 6, 7, 10, 11
Byner, Ernest 21

C

Carrier, Mark 25
Carson, Bud 22, 23
Central Division 14, 21
Cincinnati Bengals 14, 25
Collier, Blanton 11
Collins, Gary 11, 12

D

Dallas Cowboys 24, 25
Davis, Mike 15
Denver Broncos 21
Dixon, Hanford 21

E

Eastern Division 9, 12
Elway, John 21

F

Feacher, Ricky 15
Franklin Field 8

G

Graham, Otto 4, 6-11, 18
Gregg, Forest 15
Groza, Lou "The Toe" 9, 12

H

Hoard, Leroy 23, 25

J

Jones, Dub 9

K

"Kardiac Kids" 16
Kelly, Leroy 14
Kosar, Bernie 20-24

L

Langhorne, Reggie 22
Lavelli, Dante 8, 9
Los Angeles Rams 8, 10

M

Mack, Kevin 21-23
Matthews, Clay 21, 23
Metcalf, Eric 22, 25
Minnifield, Frank 21, 23
Modell, Art 11, 15, 28
Moseley, Mark 21
Motley, Marion 8, 9
Municipal Stadium 10

N

National Football League (NFL) 14
Nelson, Bill 14
New England Patriots 26
New York Giants 12
Newsome, Ozzie 15, 21
Novacek, Jay 25

P

Payton, Walter 12
Perry, Michael Dean 23
Philadelphia Eagles 8
Philcox, Todd 23, 25
Pittsburgh Steelers 27
playoffs 15, 23, 26
Pruitt, Greg 15
Pruitt, Mike 15

R

Rucker, Reggie 15
Rutigliano, Sam 15, 16
Ryan, Frank 11, 14
Rypien, Mark 25

S

Schottenheimer, Marty 16
Shofner, Jim 23
Sipe, Brian 15, 16, 19
Slaughter, Webster 21, 22
Speedie, Mac 9
St. Louis Cardinals 12
Stover, Matt 25
Super Bowl 4, 22, 26

T

Testaverde, Vinny 4, 24-28
Tomczak, Mike 23

U

United States Football League (USFL) 16
University of Miami 20

W

Warfield, Paul 11, 14